THE MAGIC LILY PAD

By the same author:

THE CURSE OF THE AZTEC DUMMY: A Nebraskan Chronicle

IS THE MOON THE CENTER OF THE UNIVERSE?

HISTORY OF RUSSIA & THE SOVIET UNION in Humorous Verse

MAKE MARZIPAN, NOT WAR: Crazy Rhymes for Crazy Times

CHEESE PIRATES: Humorous Rhymes for Adult Children

CAFÉ BOMBSHELL: The International Brain Surgery Conspiracy

PETS OF THE GREAT DICTATORS & Other Works

See excerpts at www.newacademia.com

THE MAGIC LILY PAD

AND OTHER STORIES FOR CHILDREN

by Sabrina Ramet
Artwork by Christine Hassenstab
& Sabrina Ramet

Washington, DC

New Academia Publishing, 2023

Printed in the United States of America

Library of Congress Control Number: 2023910855
ISBN 979-8-9875893-3-5 hardcover (alk. paper)

THESPRING is an imprint of New Academia Publishing

New Academia Publishing
4401-A Connecticut Ave. NW #236, Washington DC 20008
info@newacademia.com - www.newacademia.com

For Carl and Svetlana,
and their children,
Sasha and Elenora

CONTENTS

ACKNOWLEDGMENTS

I am grateful to my life partner, Christine Marie Hassenstab, for her feedback on this text, as well as for preparing some of the artwork included herein. I am also grateful to Kristian Bernhof Ellinggard for technical assistance with the final proofs. As ever, I celebrate the love and support I have enjoyed from Chris, with whom I have shared my life for more than three decades.

Sabrina Ramet
Saksvik, Norway
2 June 2023

For Children Ages 6-10

CHARLIE, MY LITTLE BIRD FRIEND

Many years ago, I had a friend who was a seagull, a beautiful white bird with a bright yellow beak. I first met him one early summer day when I was strolling on the beach, looking for seashells that had washed up on the shore. I was just picking up a pink and white conch. That is the kind of sea shell which, when you place it against your ear, gives a sound much like that of the ocean. As I bent down to pick it up, I heard the happy sound of a seagull flapping his wings. He hovered above me for a while and then found a pole near me on which to perch. "Hello," I said to this fine creature.

He gave me a soft squawk in reply.

"I shall call you Charlie," I suggested. "Is that OK?"

Another soft squawk told me that the seagull had accepted my suggestion.

Charlie and I sat around together for just five minutes or so on that day. He must have had an appointment somewhere else, because he suddenly looked quite distracted and then flew off in a rush.

I returned the next day, at the same time, to the spot where I had met Charlie, hoping that he would return. I was so happy when he floated down and landed on his perch. "Hello, Charlie," I called out, and he returned my greeting. I figured that this bird had other engagements, but before he left I promised to return the next day. I also told him that I would wear a yellow hat, so that he could easily recognize me from high up.

I returned on the third day, this time sporting a bright yellow hat and waited near the familiar pole. I was there scarcely a minute before Charlie arrived. We had a lot to talk about. Of course, I had only a rough idea what he meant by his various squawks, but he was certainly holding up his side of the conversation. I also suspect that he had only a rough idea about what I was telling him. I told him that I was a pupil at the local elementary school, enjoying my summer break – he squawked in acknowledgment – and that I liked to play baseball – Charlie squawked warmly in approval. I guessed that he liked to watch baseball games. We continued like this for weeks on end, meeting every day, as good friends can do.

Fortunately, I had been coming to the seaside early in the morning. So when it was time for school to resume, I could still stop to wait for Charlie, at our agreed time, on the way to school. For several weeks into the school year, we continued to meet and to discuss what was on our minds. But then one day he wasn't there. Had he already flown south for the winter, I wondered.

I continued to come to "the perch", as I had started calling our meeting point, for another couple of weeks. Then I decided to wait until warm weather would return.

I remember the day the following spring when I saw the skies dense with birds of various stripes. So I rushed down to the seaside the next morning, heading over to the perch. To my delight, Charlie was already there, squawking happily to see me. We continued to meet on an almost daily basis – there was an outing to the mountains with my parents that summer – for several months. And then it was time for Charlie to fly south again for his winter holiday.

This continued for another four or five years, by which time I was starting secondary school. I saw Charlie for the last time one September, when a flock of his fellow seagulls stopped by. He squawked his usual "farewell" and then left with his friends. As he flew up, he turned to me with one last and, I thought, somewhat sad squawk. I never saw him again, even though I made several visits to the perch the following summer. Where he ended up I don't know. But he gave me the gift of friendship and of happy memories of time spent together. I shall always treasure these memories.

THE MAGIC LILY PAD AND THE PICKERELWEEDS

Even an ordinary lily pad is already a very special place. Lily pads can be found at the knee-deep shallows of ponds. There, you can find small painted, spotted turtles and yellow-eyed bull frogs sitting on the larger lily pads, with dragonflies and damselflies landing on the smaller lily pads, while bees buzz around. You might even see a few beetles sunning themselves on lily pads when the weather is right. Time stands still where there are lily pads and you can literally sit there for a full day, without growing any older. You can try this some time.

On the bottom side of a lily pad you can typically find a crimson carpet, with some moss animals living there, as well as tiny snails and flatworms. Don't eat the flatworms, since they are not good for you. You might also find tiny white eggs stuck on the lily pad's underside. These belong to flattened oval insects known as whirligig beetles, that fly around at night. During the day, they rest. When they are full-grown adults, they often have a metallic green or bronze color. But you shouldn't eat these either, since they are also not good for you.

So, as you can see, there is some magic even to the typical lily pad ponds. But there is a pond high in the mountains, where condors fly by, which is special. Here the pickerelweeds glow at night (and sometimes by day) and the two-feet-tall cattails (they look like reeds but are not reeds) make a sound something like humming or singing. The scientists who have climbed to the top of the mountain to study these cattails are not sure how or why they make this curious sound, for which some of the scientists have coined a new word. Combining the "sin" from singing with most of the word "humming", they came up with the word "sinumming". That, they say, is what the cattails do. But there is more. Intermixed with the sinumming cattails and the glowing pickerelweeds, with their five inch wide leaves and violet-blue blossoms, there are a lot of lily pads. But only one of them is magical. Scientists say that, if you can figure out which lily pad is magical and very gently rub the lily pad with your thumb, you will instantly be transported to another dimension, where you can have four wishes. Whatever you do with your first three wishes, you might want to save the fourth wish to get back to the pond where you found the magic lily pad.

WILLY THE PIGEON SAVING THE ANTS

Willy the pigeon was a kind-hearted old bird, who was admired by all the other pigeons. They respected his wisdom as well as his generosity. Whenever he found a morsel of bread or a piece of cake, he immediately cooed to the other pigeons to come and share the meal with him. Sometimes there would be a spat between a couple of pigeons, but, when this occurred, Willy could always be relied upon to act as a friendly go-between and help to sort out the problem. He was a peacemaker and a wise old bird. His feathers were, of course, classic pigeon-grey, just like the other pigeons, and he kept himself very clean, bathing in the public fountain in the town square or in the local stream.

One day, Willy was out taking his morning stroll when he noticed a group of maybe about 200 or 300 ants who were marching in a circle. They were not carrying anything or going anywhere. Ants, you see, tend to follow the ant in front of them. As long as the lead ant heads somewhere, everything is fine. But when the lead ant comes up behind the last in a line of ants following him, there can be a danger that they end up just walking around in circles until they become sick. Willy had seen this once before and knew just what to do. First, he approached the ant circle very slowly, so that he would not scare any of the little creatures. Then he cooed to them in a very friendly way, almost purring like a cat, so that they would feel relaxed and safe. And then, he took one of his legs, placed it close to the ant circle, and began to scratch the ground with his claws. This quickly got the attention of the ants, and broke up their circle. The ants had been in a kind of trance, but the wise old pigeon had woken them out of their trance. The ants shook themselves a little, to wake up, smiled at Willy with gratitude, and then got in a line to march home again. As they marched off, Willy cooed a march tune to help them keep in step.

WHY THE SUN IS HAPPY

A long long time ago, the sun was very sad.

She would wake up in the morning every day, rise in the eastern horizon, look around for friends, and find no one.

"I'm all alone," the sun said to herself (speaking English, of course). "I'm all alone."

And the sun moped around a lot.

She was so sad that heavy clouds moved in, covering her up and shutting off her sunshine.

She was shrouded in clouds for many weeks.

Then, one day, while the sun was scratching herself with solar flares, the moon made himself visible in the afternoon sky.

"Hello," said the moon. "You are very bright. You make me happy."

"Thank you, " the sun replied. "That's so nice of you. What is your name?"

"I am the moon," he answered.

"Where did you come from?"

"I've been running around the earth for as long as I can remember," the moon replied, "but I usually come out only at night."

"What is night?" the sun asked curiously.

"Night is darkness, and it is what we have when you go to sleep in the west," the moon explained. "But at night I see thousands of stars like yourself – far in the distance. Millions of light years away."

"You mean I'm not the only star?!" the sun exclaimed, grinning from ear to ear. "I thought I was all alone."

"No," the moon said. "You have lots of company, but as far as I can see you are the biggest and the brightest. You are the only star that can light me up!"

"Oh, moon!" the sun sighed. "You have made me so happy, knowing that I have so many cousins in the night sky. I hope that you will visit me again."

The moon promised to do so and since that day, he has come to visit the sun from time to time, and they have talked about many interesting things, such as when flowers bloom and how much grass sheep eat each every year.

And ever since that magical day, the sun is smiling all the time. What a happy sun!

SNOW PLAYGROUND

It snowed the other day and our entire street was covered with snow. There was snow on the rooftops, snow in the trees, snowflakes on the flowers, even some snow floating around on the lake. There was snow everywhere. And, best of all, the sun was shining, lighting up the entire neighborhood with its rays. Our cat went out onto the street and was so happy that he was racing around for at least 15 minutes, in spite of the cold. In the playground at the end of the street, children were building a snowman. There was so much snow that it was easy work.

Five children cooperated in making the snowman, and they decided to make him as tall as they were. They would have liked to make him 18 feet tall, but they could not reach that high. First they gave him feet, so that he could stand. Then they built up his legs and body, gave him strong arms and fingers, and put a twig in each hand, so that he could wave the twigs around if he would like. Then they rolled a large ball of snow for his head and planted in on a short neck between his shoulders.

After they had put on his head, little Suzie pointed out that he needed a brain. So they removed the head temporarily, opened it up, and insert a pine cone into it. They figured that a pine cone could serve as the snowman's brain. After that, it was time to put the head back – clever Wendy claimed that this was the first successful head transplant in history. Then they made ears and nose for him, and then took two rocks to serve as eyes. All he needed now was a hat and a mouth. While little Elvis went running down to his house to borrow one of his father's hats, Suzie took her index finger and carved out a mouth for the snowman.

The first thing the snowman said was, "Thank you. That feels much better."

Little Stevie's eyes opened very wide. In fact, all of the children's eyes opened wide, except for Elvis' since he had not gotten back yet. Stevie wanted to say something but was a little scared, as they all were, since none of them had thought that a snowman could talk. Finally, little Stevie screwed up his courage and said to the snowman, "I am Stevie. What is your name?"

Perhaps Stevie expected the snowman to give his name as Frosty or some such thing. Instead, he replied, "I am not sure. I think that you have to give me a name as you are my parents."

"OK," said Wendy and then, to her friends: "What do you think about calling him Mark? My uncle's name is Mark and he is a smart man." The other children agreed and just then Elvis returned with a hat.

"His name is Mark," Wendy told Elvis, and with that, Elvis crowned the snowman with a Stetson, saying, "Here you go, Mark."

Oh, Mark was so happy now. His lips curved upwards at the ends and he started to chuckle a bit.

ANTS IN PANTS

Have you ever noticed that ants usually wear pants? Probably not, unless you have looked very closely. In fact, I use a magnifying glass to examine the ants as they march by in close formation. What I have found is that most battalions of ants seem to have a fixed rule that the ants must wear pants. In some battalions, some ants wear pants and some do not. So I figure that there is no rigid dress code in those battalions. And in still other battalions, I haven't found any ants wearing pants. There are several possible theories to explain why some battalions do not have any ants in pants. I am inclined to think that the most likely is that ants in pants-free battalions simply have not heard of pants, just as there are Eskimos in the far north who have never heard of Hawaiian shirts. Or if they have, they would not find them warm enough in the far north. I have never been so far north that I could encounter eskimos. The closest I have come is to buying a kimono for my partner. But again, eskimos don't wear kimonos, and nor do ants.

It is too cold around here most of the year for ants to visit. So, for my studies of ants, I fly to California, which has some ants, or Texas, which is teeming with ants, including some very big ones that don't wear pants. It's a pity that ants don't speak English, since I'd be interested in talking to them about their general lack of fashion sense and about why many of them run around completely naked. I think it would be interesting to study ants in cold climates and also in very hot climates. I think the ones in hot climates might like to stay in the shade as much as possible. I have a neighbor who says that he talks with ants. In fact, I have seen him do so. But the ants don't talk back to him. So I think his effort is wasted. Thinking about ants and watching them is very rewarding. If you haven't done any of that up to now, I can recommend that you start watching them.

SALLY AND THE TALKING OAK

Brave Sally liked to go to the woods and explore. There were many places in the woods that she liked, but her favorite place was a clearing in front of a large oak tree. She loved that oak tree and often admired its thick, crusty bark. She liked to sit beneath its leafy branches and just let her mind wander. One day, being in a particularly happy mood, she said out loud, "You lovely tree! I just love you so much!"

To her surprise, she heard the tree reply, "I love you too. You visit me regularly and I am always glad to see you."

Sally was silent for a moment, while she thought about the curious fact that she thought that she had just heard a tree talk to her. Finally, she asked the obvious question: "Do you have a name?"

"Of course, I do," the handsome oak replied. "It's Frederick. But my friends call me Freddy."

"Freddy, OK," muttered Sally, still trying to absorb the fact that she was having a conversation with a talking tree. "My name is Sally." After another pause, she asked, "Do you have friends around here?"

"All the trees I can see are friends of mine," Freddy replied.

"And they all have names, right?"

"Yes, of course they do. Some have male names and some have female names. And we talk about many things, such as sunshine and rain, clouds and clear skies, the birds that land on our branches and sing to us, and of course the children who visit us."

"It sounds like a lovely life," thought Sally out loud, "but do you have any worries? Do you ever catch the flu or get a fever?"

"Well," Freddy explained, "I'm a tree, not a human being. So my worries are not the same as yours. Around here, we trees don't get the flu, but we sometimes get lichen stuck on us. The lichen set up shop on our bark and it sometimes tickles. Fortunately for me, I've been lichen-free for several years." Then, after a pause, Freddy asked, "Do you have any dreams, any hopes for the future?"

"Yes," admitted Sally. "I want to be a superhero and rescue people from dangerous situations."

"But you are just a little girl," Freddy observed. "How will you manage that?"

"I am training my body and my mind," Sally responded, slightly irritated but also with a hint of pride. "And I have already rescued a cat from a tree."

"Obviously an unfriendly tree," Freddy noted.

"What about you, Freddy? Do you have any dreams?"

"Interesting thing, Sally. I too want to be a superhero!"

"But you are just a tree," Sally pointed out.

"I have strong roots, powerful branches, a trunk that reaches high above the other trees around here, and I have my own dreams of glory."

"I guess everyone has dreams," Sally replied.

"I certainly hope so," said Freddy.

"May your dreams all come true!"

"And also yours!"

THE MISSING TERMINAL

Pauline and Timothy had come to Chicago O'Hare International Airport with their parents. They had a three-hour lay-over, so their parents told them to run off and amuse themselves. Pauline spied a map of the airport and the two youngsters went over to it and started to study it. The words "you are here" in bright red letters told them that they were in Terminal 3. As they continued to study the map, they quickly identified Terminals 1, 2, and 5. But for the life of them, they could not locate Terminal 4 on the map. Where was Terminal 4? they wondered.

"I think the people who made this map made a mistake," offered Timmy. "If there is a Terminal 5, there has to be a Terminal 4."

"Not necessarily," Pauline replied. "Perhaps the builders had a sense of humor."

"A sense of humor when building an airport?!?" Timmy protested.

"Or maybe what goes on in Terminal 4 is so secret that its very existence is denied," Pauline offered. "Sort of the way the military denies that any extraterrestrial bodies were found at Roswell in 1947."

"I like that theory," Timmy said. "But what might they be doing down there?" Timmy had already decided that a secret terminal had to be below ground.

"Maybe that's where they construct experimental aircraft, with anti-gravity propulsion."

"Or it could be that Terminal 4 houses a huge factory manufacturing top-secret military aircraft," suggested Timmy.

"Or maybe," Pauline offered, "they could have extraterrestrials down there, working on top secret projects."

"I like that idea," Timmy replied. But then, with his left eyebrow flickering with fear, he continued, "but maybe it is a prison complex where they lock up disobedient children and naughty parents."

"Don't say that! It could just be missing," Pauline said. And with that, Pauline and Timmy scampered off to Airport Lost and Found, to report the missing terminal.

TERMINAL 3
Terminals 1-2
Terminal 5
LOST & FOUND
TERMINAL 4
Terminal 3

WELCOME TO "WE WANT"!

In Minnesota, where cats glisten at night and where farmers have reported seeing their farm animals flying around at dusk, there is a town called We Want, population just under 2,000. No one seems to remember any longer how the town got its name, although one thing's for sure: everyone or almost everyone wants something. Little Mikey wants a new bicycle for Christmas. Little Kathy wants a new doll for her birthday. Mother wants the local shop to sell fresh fish. Father wants new eye glasses, so that he can read the local newspaper. Grandpa just wants peace and quiet, since there is too much noise for his tastes. And grandma wants Saint Jezabel the weight-lifter to visit her just once.

But none of this offers any clue as to what the founders of We Want wanted. Perhaps they just wanted the land on which they built We Want. Or maybe they wanted to put a stop to the awful pollution from the nearby town of We Pollute. Or maybe they weren't quite sure what they wanted, and merely knew that there were always things one could want.

LITTLE JIMMY'S WISHES

"I wish I could be a giraffe, with a long neck, so that I could see over crowds," said little Jimmy one day. His friend Zelda heard him and told him that he would not fit into his parents' house if he became a giraffe. But already by the next day, he had changed his mind.

"I wish I could be a mountain goat," said little Jimmy, "so that I could easily climb up steep mountain slopes." Zelda listened to this, but did not say anything.

The next day, he had a different idea: "I wish I could be a California condor, so that I could fly over the mountains and beaches."

Two days later, little Jimmy thought that he might like to be a beaver: "I think that building dams on rivers must be great," he mused, "working with a team of fellow beavers. I wish I could be a beaver."

A few days later, he had another idea. Watching fireflies flying around, he marveled at how their butts lit up like light bulbs and was sure that that was fun. But his fascination with fireflies was soon eclipsed by a newfound delight in alligators. "If I were an alligator," he realized out loud, "I could lie in the sun motionless and no one would bother me, and I would be fed at 4 o'clock." He had visited the local Alligator Farm, and the alligators there were all fed at 4 o'clock every day.

"If you were an alligator," little Zelda pointed out, "we would not be friends. Alligators are boring."

"OK," replied little Jimmy. "Then I wish I could be a peacock or a bird of paradise, with colorful feathers to delight you."

"But Jimmy," wise little Zelda said now. "I like you just the way you are. It is great that you see so much beauty and grace in other species. But you can stand on stilts if you want to look over crowds, you can put on your climbing boots and hike on mountain slopes with me, we can go out in the evening with flashlights and wave them around (just like fireflies), we can get in a hot air balloon and see everything just as a condor does, and, if you want to build a little dam – well, that is something we can do together."

"What about lying around like alligators, not doing anything at all? That should be simple," little Jimmy pointed out.

"We can go to the beach," little Zelda replied, "put on some sun tan lotion and lie around just like alligators. We can do many things, and even do them together."

LITTLE MERCEDES' AUTOBIOGRAPHY AND DREAMBOAT

My name is Mercedes and I am six years old. My parents named me after their car. I am happy that they own a Mercedes and not a Dodge or a BMW. I would not like my fellow students to be calling me "BMW". They told me once that they almost bought a Toyota. I suppose it would have been OK if I had been called "Toyota", but I like my actual name. My daddy sells lawn mowers and my mommy is a travel agent. We live in a big house, with a living room, a breakfast room, a kitchen, a bathroom, a bedroom for them, and then there is my room. We also have a garage, a dog called Muppet, and a cat. We have had the cat for four years but we are still arguing about what to call the cat. I want to call it Pancake, but my parents don't like that name.

We live in Oklahoma. Our state is full of gardens. We visited Texas once, we almost visited Mexico. But then we didn't. We like to eat tacos and tostadas at the local Mexican restaurant. The restaurant has a live band that plays Mexican music. I hope that we can visit California sometime, and maybe Montana. I hear that there are still cowboys and cowgirls in Montana. When I grow up I want to be a writer and to write exciting novels that people will buy and read and give as gifts to their friends. When I grow up I want to have a cat with an agreed name. I started school in September. We have 28 students in my class and Mrs. Daisy – I forget her family name – is a nice teacher, even though she wears glasses. My best grades so far are for geography, history, and math. I wish that we had a class on astronomy, but Mrs. Daisy says that we don't study astronomy in first grade. Maybe next year.

I have started gathering wood to make a dreamboat. I have made a few sketches how to build it. I can't start building it until I have more wood. But I am working on my plans. Every night I have fun dreams. If I had a dreamboat, I could revisit the dreams I like most, and visit new dreams before I dream them. I could also travel to far away planets and talk with the people who live on them. My parents say that people on other planets won't look like us and might not speak English. But everywhere I have been in Oklahoma, people speak English. So I am sure that English is spoken everywhere in the universe. I mentioned this to Mrs. Daisy and she just smiled and gave me a wink and put her finger to her lips, as if I had discovered a special secret known only to a few people on earth. I want to be an astronaut and fly on missions to other planets. And also write novels, as I already said. And be a good person. Most of all I want to be a good person. And I don't want to repeat myself too much. Grandpa repeats himself all the time, and it gets boring. I don't want to be boring. Daddy says that in Mexico most people speak both English and Spanish. Maybe I should study Spanish, just in case people on other planets speak Spanish better than English. Next year I start second grade!

THE SUBMARINE THAT CHASED A CAR

Bad Bob robbed Lucille's chocolate shoppe on Mission Street. He didn't take any money and he didn't harm her. But you can only imagine her surprise when Bad Bob walked into her shoppe holding a large sack and a water pistol, and demanded that she fill his sack with chocolates. Lucille was more amused, in a way, than afraid. But, of course, she was not so happy about giving her chocolates away free of charge. "Are those all for you?" she asked, "or will you give some of them to deserving children?" "Mine, all mine," Bad Bob replied, as he walked quickly out of Lucille's chocolate shoppe.

Lucille immediately called the police, but she was told that all the police were busy with more important things to do than round up a chocolate bandit. She was frustrated now, but then she remembered that she had a friend who was the captain of a submarine. His name was Captain Madison, just like the name of our fourth president. She had seen Bad Bob get into his bright red Chevrolet, with black stripes on each side, and speed away. She gave Captain Madison the details and he promised to help her.

The captain's first move was to contact the local television station, to have them send up a helicopter to follow Bad Bob's bright red Chevrolet. The helicopter was sent up quickly, piloted by Rocket Henry, who reported to Captain Madison that Bad Bob was driving down Highway One heading south, in the direction of Santa Cruz. Downtown Santa Cruz is lovely and sits on the edge of a popular beach. But Bad Bob was not interested in sunning himself on the beach, or in walking the forest trails near Santa Cruz. On the contrary, he continued driving until he reached Monterey and then continued driving south. Captain Madison kept pace, relying on Rocket Henry to report Bad Bob's current location and, as Bad Bob reached Paso Robles, famed for its art galleries and coffee houses, Captain Madison was at his flank, just off the coast of that same city. Pismo Beach, where Russians gather to write letters home, was his next destination and this time, he had to stop at a gas station to get fuel and more chocolates. As he got out of his car, he spied the helicopter hovering above and wondered to himself if he was being followed. No matter: he got back in his car and pressed the accelerator hard, driving just one mile an hour less than legally permitted on Highway One. Before long, he reached Solvang, a Danish village with just over 5,000 inhabitants. Solvang is very picturesque and everything looks very Danish, but Bad Bob did not stop but continued driving another 40 minutes until he reached Santa Barbara, with its famously beautiful Spanish mission and famed for having more restaurants per capita than any other city in the United States. He considered stopping for a dinner at one of that city's finer restaurants, but, when he saw the helicopter still hovering above him, he decided to continue to drive and to try to elude the helicopter. He headed to Los Angeles, certain that, with plenty of other red cars on the road, he could elude the helicopter. He was not aware, of course, that the helicopter was not really chasing him, it was merely keeping tabs on his location so that the submarine could follow him. He drove through Los Angeles and headed down to Mission San Juan Capistrano. Here he decided to take a break, got dinner, walked around the mission grounds, even inspecting the small rooms where the monks used to live, and bought a few postcards. He saw the helicopter hovering over the mission during his visit but started to think that it was meaningless.

After dinner and postcards, he got back in his car and continued to drive south. His destination was San Diego, where he had moored his pleasure boat. He drove down to the waterfront, got out of his car, and walked casually over to his boat, with his sack of chocolates slung over his shoulder. He got into his pleasure boat, which was already loaded down with lots of chocolates from previous thefts, untied the lines mooring his boat in place, started the motor and began to speed away. As he sailed out onto open water, Captain Madison brought his submarine to the surface and sent his crew onto the pleasure boat to arrest Bad Bob and bring him to justice. The moral of this story? Chocolates are tasty on a tray, but remember that crime does not pay.

MUSIC INSIDE A COCONUT

Millie was mulling over an idea that she had about traveling to other planets when she looked up and saw that there were coconuts in the coconut tree. Just then, her friend Mickey meandered over to where she was mulling. He saw that she was looking up at the coconut tree and so he started to do the same. Soon Henry and Harriet looped along, stopped in their tracks when they saw Millie and Mickey looking up, and joined them. Now there were four children looking up at the top of the coconut tree, occasionally emitting an impressed "Ah…." or, every now and then, a more dramatic "Ooooh!"

After they had been standing there staring upwards for maybe 15 minutes, Farmer Ferdy came along, as usual with a sack of potatoes slung over his shoulder. Farmer Ferdy was very strong and he could carry very large sacks of potatoes. He was also very talkative and asked the children what they were looking at.

"We are looking at the coconuts," replied Millie, since she had been the first to arrive on the scene and thought that she was therefore entitled to speak for the entire group. Besides, what she said was true: the four children were looking at the coconuts.

"They are very high up," Farmer Ferdy observed.

"Yes they are," said Mickey smartly. "And we cannot see much detail."

"Ah," said Farmer Ferdy in response. "You would like to see detail. Well, let me fetch my ladder and perhaps I can bring a coconut down for you to see."

With that, the farmer laid down his burden at the base of the coconut tree and sauntered off in the direction of his farmhouse. Some minutes passed but eventually Farmer Ferdy returned with his ladder, set it up near the coconut tree, and climbed up to the very highest step. He stretched out his arm to reach one of the coconuts, but it was just a little bit out of reach. So he came down the ladder, scratched his head, and said to the children, "We'll have to find another solution."

With that, he took his ladder and carried it back to his farmhouse. The children continued to stare upwards. Soon the farmer was back, this time with a lasso. He spread his legs apart to steady himself and then began to twirl the lasso around until he was ready to hurl it upwards. He missed. But he tried again, and on his second try, he brought down a large hairy coconut and presented it to the children. "Here you are," he said, a little proud of himself for his lassoing skill.

Millie and Mickey held the coconut in their hands, while Henry and Harriet looked on.

"What a beautiful coconut," Harriet declared.

The other children all nodded in agreement. The coconut was trembling a little. Instinctively, Millie put it to her ear and then announced, "There's music inside this coconut!"

"Is it a band? Is it march music?" Somehow, Henry's first thought was of marches.

"No, that's not it," said Millie.

"Perhaps it's a jazz piano," suggested Harriet tentatively. From the look on her face, it was clear that she was hoping for something magical.

"No," said Millie, "nothing like a piano. And probably not jazz either."

"May I listen?" Mickey asked politely, and Millie passed the coconut to him.

"Yes," Mickey said, confirming Millie's judgment. "There is definitely music inside this coconut, but not like anything I have heard before, and definitely not a miniature rock group." Why Mickey thought it was useful to rule out the possibility that there might be a miniature rock group performing inside the coconut has never been explained. He handed the coconut back to Millie.

As Millie put the coconut once more against her ear, her eyes grew wide and she exclaimed, "I think there's a bee trapped inside the coconut!"

"Shall we release it?" kind Farmer Ferdy asked.

Millie handed the coconut to Farmer Ferdy, who placed the musical miracle against his ear. He quickly confirmed her conclusion: "Yes, there's a bee trapped inside the coconut! Let's liberate it."

And with that, he pulled out the hammer he always kept in his hip pocket, placed the coconut on the ground, and gave it a whack. With that, the coconut split open and out flew not just one bee but four or five of them, who, after thanking the farmer and the children for freeing them from captivity, immediately flew off in search of flowers. The children, and Farmer Ferdy too, were left to wonder how it had happened that the bees got trapped inside a coconut. They developed a few theories, but never really figured out how something so strange could have happened. Have *you* ever found a coconut with bees trapped inside? I hope you released them.

MY CAT'S TRILINGUAL

My cat is very very smart. He knows, for instance, that sitting patiently and staring at me is a better way to get me to open the door for him than meowing. It is also a better way than meowing to get me to invite him onto my lap for a cuddle. But what does he want now precisely? It could be either of these things. Of course, sometimes he does speak and I have seen for myself that he is trilingual. He speaks cat languages and he has a separate language for speaking to me. For example, in talking to other cats, he sometimes snarls, sometimes hisses, and seems to have a wide vocabulary to say "Get off my property!" That seems to be his main concern in talking with other cats. He never snarls or hisses at me, and he happily allows that his property is also my property.

But in talking to me and also to my honey, he has a much wider range of intonation and word choice. A soft little meow, barely audible, means "I love you." A confused meow means "I just woke up and I'm not sure what I want." A short hissy-fit meow means that I left him outside longer than he wanted to be, and that he thinks that I should have checked on him sooner. A short meow without emotion means that he wants to go outside. When he wants to be fed, he just comes and sits in front of me saying nothing. This is rare, however, because I feed him regularly and, in the morning, he gets breakfast in bed – which is to say before he is fully awake.

It took a while before I realized that our cat was trilingual, but then I detected a unique speech pattern when he talks to birds. I realized that the only thing he says to small birds that fly in our garden is "Come down a little lower, so that I can catch you." Although he does not say that to other cats, perhaps his sentence for birds can be seen as part of a language for other animals, cats and birds and, if the occasion ever arose, perhaps also for dogs.

Probably some other cats are also trilingual. But one thing I know for sure: my cat is one of the smartest cats on the planet. The proof of this is his mediation in neighborhood disputes. The first time this happened involved two other cats hissing and snarling at each other. Our kitty went up to them, meowed a few times forcefully but convincingly, and then listened to their respective complaints. He then meowed a few more times in what sounded like an explanatory mode and, after just a couple of minutes, the two cats wandered off in separate directions, apparently reconciled and content. More surprising was another act of mediation in which Kitty involved himself a couple of weeks later, when a neighbor was scolding his own cat. Although it was none of his business, Kitty decided to see what he could do to help. He went up to the two of them and, if I am interpreting his meows accurately, he asked each of them what the dispute was about. I was sitting on my balcony and, thus, at a distance and, therefore, could not hear what the neighbor was saying. All I can report is that the neighbor gave Kitty his version of things, and the neighbor cat gave Kitty her version. Kitty then thought about this for a bit, and then started his mediation, going back and forth between the two. Of course, it is perhaps not so remarkable that the two cats found a common language. But I was quite impressed that the neighbor seemed to understand the basic point being made by Kitty. By the time Kitty finished his work, the neighbor was stroking his cat, and his cat was cuddling up to his leg.

Now I am wondering if Kitty could get involved in international mediation, reconciling the US and Russia, and creating a happy atmosphere all over the world. Certainly, if anyone could do this, it would be our Kitty.

UNICORN IN MY DREAMS

When I sleep, I always dream and all of my dreams are happy dreams. Some of them are even magical. I often dream about unicorns. Unicorns are always white. Some people claim to have seen orange or blue unicorns, but have never presented any photos. Everyone knows that unicorns are white and have golden horns.

In my dreams I am riding a unicorn. We fly high above my garden. Did you know that unicorns can fly? We fly through the clouds, which sparkle yellow and pink. These are my favorite colors. Actually, all the colors are my favorites. There are two colors that I see in my dreams that I never see when I am awake. You may think of one of these as blue- and copper-colored at the same time and sparkling. The other color is hard for me to describe. I think of it as some sort of pink, but it is not pink at all, nothing like pink. More like yellow.

Back to the unicorn. I call him Horace, after the uncle I never had. Horace-the-unicorn flies me to magical places – to forests of ferns with small brooks running through them, to enormous tulip fields, to canals with gondolas, to the clouds of Venus, even to Mars. One night we flew over Saturn's rings. They looked like a runway to me, but Horace-the-unicorn told me that there was no solid runway strip on the rings. So we continued our journey to Jupiter before returning to my bed. One of these nights I hope that we can fly to Pluto. I know it's a bit cold on Pluto, but I have a warm jacket. Horace, being magical, does not have to worry about the cold. I'm going to lie down now in preparation for my next flight with Horace.

THE SMILING LEAF

In my garden there is a tall dogwood tree. (I've never understood why it's called dogwood, since my dog treats it the same way as he treats any other tree, if you know what I mean.) Anyway, every weekday, when I walk to school, I pass the dogwood tree and I always notice a certain leaf smiling at me. No, it doesn't have a mouth or lips but, all the same, it is clearly smiling at me. So I smile back at the leaf and the leaf seems very happy at this.

I've thought a lot about the smiling leaf on my dogwood tree. And I have lots of questions. Of course, I don't need to ask where it comes from, as I sometimes do with people I meet, since it is part of the tree. But I wonder if it smiles at me because it is happy to see me, or does it smile all the time? Also, why don't any of the other leaves smile? Are they grumpy? And how to communicate with a leaf? With my brain waves?

Well, I don't need to figure all of this out today. In fact, it's probably OK if these questions join certain other questions in my head, questions to which I don't yet have answers.

For Persons 11 or Older

DO MY GOLDFISH HAVE SHORT MEMORIES?

I am worried. In fact, I have been worried for a long time. My goldfish, seven in all, don't look right. They swim around but show no recognition of me at all. I have tried to introduce myself, as one might to goldfish in a tank, pressing my face up against the tank and smiling broadly. But they just dash away and hide in the corner, as if they had never seen me before. I have tried singing to them as I put their fish food into the water. They take the food, of course, but don't respond to my singing and don't show any particular sign of gratitude. When I feed my cat, my cat purrs and cuddles up to me. So I can say that I know that my cat does not have any memory problems. But my fish neither purr nor cuddle up. I know, you will say that they are in the fish tank and I am outside; so there is no way that they can cuddle up to me. But that is only one way of looking at the issue. They could, for example, cuddle up to the glass or wink at me or even cuddle with each other. But they don't do any of these things.

My goldfish always have their eyes wide open but open and shut their mouths rhythmically, while staring blankly. Are all goldfish like this or is it just my goldfish who have this blank look on their faces? My goldfish never smile, they never look angry or sad or frustrated. There is no sign that they make jokes among themselves, or that they quarrel with each other or tell stories. Whether swimming around in circles endlessly qualifies as relaxing, I don't know. But they don't look particularly relaxed, just bored. Or maybe not even bored because, to be bored, you have to have some mental activity going on, you have to feel that you can imagine something better. I doubt that my goldfish can imagine anything better. And if you object that they are not free and that I should take them to a freshwater stream and toss them in, just ask yourself how long these little morsels would last in the world outside. And, you know what?, I think they would be just the same in the wild.

In high school, we all had to dissect frogs, against our protests, but I have never dissected a goldfish. Nor would I want to do so. But I think that I can say with some assurance that their brains must be pretty small to fit into their tiny heads. So probably there is not much room for thinking about anything besides continuing to swim in circles, looking for food, and trying to avoid bumping into their fellow fish. I'm glad I'm not a goldfish.

THE PENGUIN CONVENTION

Penguins love conventions. They love to dress up in their best suits and get together with other penguins, huddling close, whispering to each other, and sharing their views. Some of them even present academic papers.

Not all penguin conventions are the same, of course. There was a convention a few years ago organized by a group of vegetarian penguins who wanted to persuade other penguins to give up eating fish and squids and, yes, shrimp-like krill too. That didn't get anywhere, with plenty of penguins pointing out to these vegetarians that there might not be enough moss in the Antarctic to feed all the fish-loving penguins. And none of the penguins were keen on eating moss.

But three years ago the penguins held a most bizarre convention. Some penguins had been watching the Discovery Channel and had found out that there were polar bears living in the Arctic. This might seem a matter of no consequence for Antarctic-bound penguins, except that those who had seen the program on the Discovery Channel became obsessed with the idea of persuading the polar bears to move south, so that polar bears and penguins could be neighbors. There could even be an advantage for the bears, since much of their habitat in the north is gradually but steadily melting away. A long debate ensued on how to persuade them to move and how the bears could pull off this feat. The convention lasted five days, but broke up with no clear resolution regarding the polar bears.

But last year's convention, convened as usual in late spring, was – one might say—historic. The penguins had become more than aware that the climate locally was changing. Where there had once been hills of ice and snow, there were now only large mounds of moss. The penguins didn't like that and, after a probing discussion, they decided to march to Washington D.C. to present their case. They knew that this would be a long trek, but they were full of determination. They didn't need to have everyone march; so they decided that twenty of their number would make the journey.

Normally getting from their continent to Tierra del Fuego might have been a problem. But there were huge icebergs splitting off and drifting northward. So the penguin deputation – twenty in all – jumped onto one of these icebergs as it broke off and started their trip. Unfortunately they thought at first, but actually fortunately, their iceberg missed Tierra del Fuego and drifted northward along the coast of Argentina, finally docking in Buenos Aires. So it was from the Argentine capital that they started their march, singing penguin songs as they went their way. They sang so loudly that the penguins in the Buenos Aires Ecopark, all 12 of them, hopped out and waddled at full speed to catch up with the penguin deputation and join their ranks.

It was the same in Montevideo, where the nine penguins in residence at Parque Lecocq flapped their wings in excitement and likewise waddled at full speed to join the other penguins.

As they continued on their way through Rio de Janiero, Sao Paolo, Caracas, Bogota, and several of the cities of Central America, swimming in the Atlantic whenever it was mealtime, their ranks continued to grow until, by the time they reached Mexico, there were more than 600 penguins marching, singing, and, of course, eating fish and krill along the way.

Their timing had been lucky because, by the time they reached the Mexican border, it was already October and the temperature was going down. They continued to alternate between marching and swimming along the coast, reaching New Orleans in time for one of the city's Mardi Gras parades. As the now more than 900 penguins joined the parade, they were cheered by onlookers, some of them shouting "Power to the penguins!" or perhaps a bit mysteriously, "Penguins are always right!"

And so it went, until one sunny but mild day in early April, this massive force of now more than 1,400 penguins reached Washington D.C., marching straight up to the Congress. They seemed to know instinctively that they needed to address both houses of Congress and demanded a joint session. The majority leaders in both the House and the Senate agreed and immediately called a joint session of Congress. So, the very next day, the penguins marched into the Great Hall. The chief sergeant-at-arms gave them a warm welcome, and the congressmen and congresswomen were entirely fascinated.

The penguins marched up to the front of the Great Hall with their chief spokespenguin taking the podium. Then, with calm precision, they explained to the Congress what was happening to their habitat, how they were losing their beautiful ice castles and how they were worried about their future, especially about the younger generation of penguins. They made their case so convincingly that congressmen and congresswomen alike started to sob and decided then and there to put a stop to the burning of fossil fuels, to ban the use of cars using gasoline, and to get to work to reverse global warming. It was a great victory for the penguins and for the whole world. We can all thank the penguins for saving the planet!

After that victory, the penguins continued their march northward until they reached the Arctic and greeted the polar bears. When the penguins told the polar bears what they had accomplished, the bears were pleased and they decided to have a banquet to celebrate. The polar bears ate seal fat and the penguins ate seafood, and they made a lot of sounds that might have been singing.

HYPNOTIZING GOATS

At one time, the army had a program to hypnotize goats. The idea was to put the goats in a hypnotic trance and get them to engage in remote viewing, meaning that they would "see" top secret military bases in enemy countries. The army officers were convinced that goats were potentially ideal for this assignment and would be able to "see" objects as far away as 6,000 miles, and in great detail.

So the first thing to do was to give the goats a battery of intelligence tests, so that only the brightest goats would be selected for this program. They tested about 120 goats, hoping to see which of them were the fastest in kicking square pegs into square holes and round pegs into round holes. In fact, the goats were not interested in kicking pegs at all – from which the army concluded that the goats were too smart for such a simple-minded game and didn't want to waste their time with it. They next tried simple math, hoping that, if the officers tapped their feet twice, waited a moment, and tapped twice more, the goats would add up the taps and tap their hoofs four times. Once again, these smart goats couldn't be bothered with such a simple test. Finally, the army administered a test involving word recognition. Given their interests, they wanted to determine which goats understood the words "military base", "surface to air missiles", "aircraft", and of course "yes" and "no". This last test was inconclusive, although some goats did a lot of bleating – whether out of frustration with the test or for some other reason.

Finally, after a short argument between army officers who wanted to choose the bleaters and those who wanted to avoid them, the decision was taken to pick 16 goats at random, taking each of them into a standard interrogation room, where each of them would be met by one army officer.

Each of the officers would try to hypnotize his goat, swinging a small silver pendulum in front of the goat's eyes, while telling the goat to relax and listen to some instructions. The officer would then tell the goat to imagine itself at a foreign military base and explain what it saw. After that, goat and officer simply stared at each other for more than an hour. The result, sorry to say, was the same in every case. When the doors were opened, the goats seemed the same as before and had nothing to bray about secret military installations in foreign lands, but – here's the twist – the officers came out on all fours, bleating and seemingly convinced that they were goats!

A STRANGE NAPKIN

I can't explain it, but every time I try to lay my napkin flat on the table it pops up and stands on its edge. I can knock it down, but it just pops up again. I can blow on it and it waves a bit but continues to stand on its edge. My neighbor thinks that this is a case of demonic possession and has offered to call a priest to carry out an exorcism. But the napkin is not doing anything evil; so I don't think that my neighbor's theory makes any sense at all. My best friend has suggested, rather, that there may be pixies with a sense of humor, working day and night to restore the napkin to an upright position. But I think that pixies have better things to do. Fairies, being supernatural beings with wings and the gift of magic, have also been offered as an explanation. But there are other possibilities too. One is that the napkins are simply strange, perhaps magnetized in some way or charged with electricity the way your hair can get if you comb it for a while. Another is that the napkins I have in my house were not in fact purchased at the local supermarket, but were placed in my house by extraterrestrials in order to distract me. I don't think this makes much sense, however, because I remember buying the napkins at the supermarket and because I am not *that* distracted by my napkins and in any event, I have not seen any extraterrestrials walking around in my house. There are probably other theories, but I am waiting for other friends to come forward with their ideas.

ONCE UPON A TIME…

Once upon a time there was a story which began with the words "Once upon a time…" Many good stories begin this way because events happen in time. If they did not happen in time, they would not happen at all. Imagine starting a story with the words "Once something happened outside of time…" It would not make sense, because things happen in time, they happen *once upon a time.* It has always been this way, ever since an old story-teller, once upon a time, started his story with the words "Once upon a time…" Since then, many story-tellers have followed in his footsteps, without remembering who the old story-teller was or when, once upon a time, the first story was written that began with the words "Once upon a time…"

THE MAN WITH TWO COATS

There was a man who had two coats. One was red, one was blue. Other than the color difference, the two coats were identical. They were both made of wool, both had the same number of buttons, neither coat had a hood, and both were reasonably warm. The man with two coats sometimes had difficulty deciding which coat to wear, since there was not much difference between them. Of course, if he was wearing a bright red shirt and, less often, red pants, he sometimes thought it was best to stick to red. But other times he thought that that would be too much red color, and then he would wear the blue coat. If he was wearing a bright blue shirt or blue pants, he sometimes thought it made sense to wear his blue coat, but sometimes he didn't think so and put on his red coat. When he wore a green shirt, this was less of a dilemma and he usually then chose the red coat. But sometimes he fancied wearing a blue coat on top of his green shirt. It all depended on his mood. Usually he was cheerful, in which case he could wear either the red coat or the blue coat; but sometimes he was a little depressed, in which case he could still wear either coat, although he might just stay at home and try to think happy thoughts, such as thoughts of waterfalls or of ferns swaying in the breeze or of a sunrise viewed from the alps or of his pet cat, who also had two coats but who, unlike her owner, never wore either of them.

It went on like this for a long time until, one day, the man with two coats took a brave decision and went out to buy a third coat – and not just any coat, but a morning coat. Of course, he knew that a morning coat would be just for the morning and, if he went out at, say, 11 in the morning wearing his morning coat, he would need to get home by noon or, at the latest 1 in the afternoon to change into one of his other coats. No, it would never do to wear a morning coat in the afternoon. People might think you were mad. But buying a morning coat was not as simple as you might think. First of all, he had to consider whether he wanted another red coat or some other color, such as blue. Or maybe take his chances with an olive green coat. And again, did he want a tight fit or a more comfortable loose fit, or just ask the shop attendant what the fashion was, so that he could do the same as everyone else? In fact, he was spending too much time thinking about these matters because the shops in London offered morning coats in only two colors – black and grey – and no shop attendant was prepared to fit him with a loose-hanging morning coat. So he did what the shop attendant told him to do and bought a rather tight-fitting grey morning coat.

Now he looked dapper! He had been a single man for many years but, when he walked out of the shop wearing his new, grey morning coat, several pretty young women immediately flocked around him, showing a lot of interest in him. They wanted to know his name, his profession, his hobbies, his opinions about politics, and whether he had a cat – which, as already mentioned, he did. His cat's name was Fuzzy. There were five young women there, all smiling at him and obviously becoming more and more delighted with his wit. So he invited them to come with him for high tea at the Savoy Hotel, overlooking the River Thames. All of them readily agreed and the six of them almost skipped to the hotel, with a couple of the ladies singing songs from "The Sound of Music". Upon arrival at the hotel, they took the lift to the top floor, where high tea was being served and sat down to enjoy cakes and biscuits, jams and scones with clotted cream. They giggled happily as they enjoyed their conversation and sipped their tea. They giggled as they ate their cakes, but tried to keep their lips together while giggling. They had such a good time that they decided to get together every week for high tea at the Savoy. And the man with three coats said to himself, "Life seems to be better now that I have a third coat."

BABY JELLYFISH'S BIG QUESTIONS

Baby jellyfish looked worried. Have you ever seen a jellyfish look worried? If you have, you know that the poor thing can look very depressed. "What is wrong, Debbie?" mama jellyfish asked her daughter.

"Mama," Debbie the jellyfish replied. "I am worried about a lot of things and I have a lot of questions."

"OK, baby," mama said, "let's start with whatever worries you the most."

"There are sharks out there, mama, and I have heard that they eat jellyfish for breakfast. I don't want to be eaten, especially not by a shark."

"You can relax, Debbie," mama responded. "Sharks only eat blue and green jellyfish. They don't eat red jellyfish. We are red. So we are safe."

"Why don't they eat us too?" asked the ever inquisitive Debbie.

"Because we are poisonous," wise old mama explained. "One bite of us and a shark's health is ruined for a long period of time. The younger sharks can die from one bite of a red jellyfish."

"Being poisonous does not sound so good, mama."

"My little jellyfish, we are not poisonous to each other, only to other species. So being poisonous is very very good."

"OK, that's good," Debbie said and then, "I have another question."

"OK, I'm all ears."

"Ears? What are those?"

"It's just an expression, Debbie. Jellyfish don't have ears. I just mean that I am ready to hear what you have to say."

"Well," little Debbie-the-jellyfish began, somewhat hesitantly, "I look around and, as far as I can see, many jellyfish look very much the same. But you have no trouble recognizing me and I always recognize you without any problem."

"That's the power of love, sweetie. To me, you are unique. You are my eldest and I love you so much."

"OK, that brings up another question. Where do I come from?"

"From right here in the Pacific Ocean."

"No, I mean how did I come about in the first place."

"Ah," replied Debbie's wise old mama. "This is where things get very interesting. Jellyfish reproduce both sexually and asexually, alternating by generation. The medusa generation reproduces sexually and the courtship of jellyfish is beautiful to observe. Jellyfish are so gentle and, when they have sex, the softness of their touch, of our touch, is most delightful. Then there is the second generation, the polyp generation, where we reproduce asexually by a process called strobilation."

"Mama, that's a big word."

"Don't worry about it, Debbie-dear. When the time comes for you, you will strobilate effortlessly."

"How old am I right now?"

"You are just two months old and, before you ask the next question, I am 8 years old."

"What's the purpose of life, mama?" Debbie asked, changing the topic without warning.

"Hmmn, that's a big question," mama jellyfish replied. "We just swim around in swarms, eating small plants and fish eggs, trying to avoid people, and humming."

"Humming?"

"Surely you have heard me hum, Debbie. Humming is the way we jellyfish have entertained ourselves for the past 650 million years."

"Mama," said little Debbie, looking admiringly at her mother, "you are so wise and so smart. Are all jellyfish as wise and smart as you are?"

"I wish they were," mama replied. "But there are lots of stupid jellyfish in the ocean. And they can get into all sorts of trouble. But you have a good nervous system and you will grow wiser and smarter as you get older."

FARMER JAKE'S FENCE

Farmer Jake had a fence. But that's putting it the wrong way. Farmer Jake had a farm, on which he had a farmhouse, in which he lived with his wife. He also had lots of farm animals, including cows, sheep, goats, horses, and pigs, as well as chickens, and a large dog of no particular breed to help him keep all of these animals orderly. And around his farmhouse he had a fence.

One day, Farmer Jake decided to give his fence a fresh coat of white paint. So he went out to his fence and did some painting, and the next day it rained. And he said to himself, "It's raining."

A few days later, after it had stopped raining and the fence was once again dry, he took his paint brush and a can of white paint and went out to do a bit more painting on his fence. And the next day it rained. And he said to himself, "That's interesting. I did some painting yesterday, and today it's raining."

He took a few days off from painting his fence and it did not rain. But when he returned to painting, again it rained the next day. Farmer Jake noticed this and told his wife that it was raining – something which she had already noticed. And he told her that he had painted the fence the day before and that every time he painted the fence, it rained the following day. His wife didn't make much of this, except to tell him, "Well, dear, the next time you need more rain, why not go out and do some more painting on the fence?!"

Farmer Jake knew that there should not be any connection between painting the fence and getting rain the following day, but this pattern continued for several months (by which time he had applied several coats of paint to his fence). It was always the same: whenever he painted, there was rain the next day and whenever he did other things and did not paint, there was no rain coming.

He decided to talk about this with the wisest man in his village – the parish priest. So he entered the confessional. This is the best way to talk to a priest because he has to stay sitting in his little compartment and has to listen to whatever you want to say to him. Farmer Jake was a bit nervous all the same because he knew that the priest would expect to hear him list some sins, like forgetting to say grace before dinner. But he went into the confessional anyway, knelt down, and began, "Bless me father, I have a fence."

"Well, my child, we all have fences," the priest replied.

"Yes, father, I suppose so," came Father Jake's rejoinder, "but are all fences magical?"

The priest took a moment to respond and then asked his parishioner, "Why do you think your fence is magical?"

"Because," Farmer Jake answered, "every time I paint it, the next day it rains."

"Hmmn," the priest replied. And then, after a moment, he said, "I absolve you of your sins. For your penance, say three Our Fathers, three Hail Marys, and three Glory Bees. Go in peace."

Farmer Jake was disappointed. The priest had not helped him sort out the apparent connection between painting and rain – no, not at all. Farmer Jake did not say any of the prayers the priest had listed; I think that this meant that the absolution did not stick. Instead, Farmer Jake drove back to his farm with the stain of unconfessed sins still on his soul and resumed painting the fence, which probably had at least six coats of paint by then. But the next day, to his astonishment, it did not rain. He could not understand this. He had done the usual amount of painting and had expected the usual amount of rain. He told his wife at the end of the day, "I painted the fence yesterday, but it has not rained today."

"Yes, dear," came his wife's helpful reply. "Maybe the angel responsible for sending rain has the day off."

This was the first time that Farmer Jake had heard of any rain angel and it seemed unlikely that spiritual beings would need to have days off. He did know what to make of this. But from that point on, there did not seem to be any consistent pattern or connection between painting the fence and getting rain. There were days when he painted and there was no rain the next day, days when he painted the fence that were followed by rain the next day, and even some days when it rained even though he had not applied any more paint to the fence the previous day. In search of an answer, he inspected his fence and he saw that the six or seven coats of paint he had given the fence had resulted in the fence having a very thick layer of white. Was there some explanation here which he could not figure out? He told his wife that he had painted the entire fence at least six times and she just replied, "Well, that's nice, dear."

He thought of going back to the confessional to tell the priest that the spell seemed to have been broken. But he figured that the priest would just tell him to recite more prayers. So he decided, instead, to talk to his goats about this. His goats always listened very attentively to everything he told them, unless they found something more interesting to do.

HECTOR, THE CHAMPION RACE HORSE

Hector was a nice horse, always polite, and always considerate of others. But he was supposed to be a race horse and he was bandy-legged. His owner, Oscar, a generally kind man but inevitably one interested in making money, was worried. Hector's trainer also had his doubts about the horse. It was hard for either of them to imagine Hector doing well at the racetrack. Oscar even started to think of sending Hector off to the glue factory. Fortunately for Hector, the owner's son, Billy, saw potential in Hector and offered to use his pocket money to hire a special trainer for Hector, one specialized in working with bandy-legged horses. Oscar was touched by his son's gesture of love for and confidence in Hector and decided to use his own money to arrange for special training for Hector, even while retaining his usual trainer for the horse.

The special training went well and, over a period of six months, Hector became steadily stronger, more sure-footed, and incredibly fast on his feet. After 10 months of special training, Oscar decided to enter Hector in a race at the Alameda racetrack. There were three races scheduled at Alameda that day: Hector was competing in the third race. The entire family – Oscar, his wife Gina, son Billy, and the two horse trainers – sat in the stands, both excited and nervous. Mainly nervous. They could hardly focus at all on the first two races and, after these first two races ended, they could not remember anything about them, not even which horse had won.

Then came time for Hector's race. Hector was one of 14 horses competing. Among them were Peanut, who had won five previous races, and Locomotive (strange name for a horse), who had won in six previous races. Oscar, Gina, and Billy looked at each other anxiously as the horses came up to the starting gate. Hector's jockey, on the other hand – Jack the Jockey – looked full of confidence. He had been training with Hector and had come to feel very close to the horse. Then the pistol was fired and the horses took off. To his family's delight, Hector shot ahead immediately, leaving even Peanut and Locomotive trailing far behind. Fans in the stand gasped with awe at Hector's speed and then went wild. Some of them compared him to lightning. Some fans would later claim that Hector broke the sound barrier, causing a sonic boom that shattered a lot of champagne glasses. But this is not true: no one was drinking champagne in the stands. Hector had won his first blue ribbon.

Three months later, there was another race – and again Hector took first place. Bandy-legged or not, Hector went on to win 28 races in a row. Finally, Oscar decided that Hector had earned a retirement in luxury and, from then on, Hector stayed at Oscar's ranch, eating the finest oats and other delicacies enjoyed by his species, giving rides to children, and helping to encourage other horses, especially those that were bandy-legged.

www.ingramcontent.com/pod-product-compliance
Lightning Source LLC
Chambersburg PA
CBHW070623310726
48982CB00001B/159
* 9 7 9 8 9 8 7 5 8 9 3 3 5 *